2605 Kewan
Dr

Ken Nicholson

GARY GEDDES

flying
blind

GOOSE LANE

© Gary Geddes, 1998.

All rights reserved. No part of this work may be reproduced or used in any form or by any means, electronic or mechanical, including photocopying, recording, or any retrieval system, without the prior written permission of the publishers.

Published in Canada by Goose Lane Editions and in England by Enitharmon Press. The publishers gratefully acknowledge the assistance of the Canada Council, the Department of Canadian Heritage, and the New Brunswick Department of Municipalities, Culture and Housing.

Author photo by Marni Craig.
Cover design by Julie Scriver.
Book design by Ryan Astle.
Printed in Canada by Hignell Book Printing.

10 9 8 7 6 5 4 3 2 1

Canadian Cataloguing-in-Publication Data

Geddes, Gary, 1940-
    Flying Blind

        Poems.
        ISBN 0-86492-232-9

1. Title.

PS8563.E3F59 1998   C811' .54   C98-950069-1
PR9199.3.G4F59 1998

British Library Cataloguing-in-Publication Data

A catalogue record for this book is available from the British Library.
ISBN 1-900564-26-2

Enitharmon Press   Distributed in Europe by
36 St George's Avenue   Littlehampton Book Services
London   N7 OHD   through Signature Book Representation
ENGLAND   2 Little Peter Street
                                Manchester   M15 4PS
                                ENGLAND

Goose Lane Editions
469 King Street
Fredericton, New Brunswick
CANADA E3B 1E5

for John Asfour
and Larry (Freeman) Flynn

CONTENTS

Acknowledgements

"High Ground," "If" and "Grouse" were awarded second prize in the *Stand Magazine* International Poetry Competition. "On Reading Akio Chida's Translations" and "Dances with Coyotes" won prizes, respectively, in the Bridport and Leacock Poetry Competition. "The Prize" was shortlisted for the Guy Owen Prize at the University of North Carolina, "The Quality of Light" for the National Poetry Competition, and portions of "Flying Blind" for the Pablo Neruda Prize in Tulsa, Oklahoma. Poems from *Flying Blind* have appeared in *Orbis, The Ottawa Citizen, Nimrod, Southern Poetry Review, The Bridport Anthology, Southerly, Stand Magazine, Parchment,* and *Take This Waltz* (edited by Ken Norris). I want to thank the editors of these magazines and books, as well as the Canada Council, the Ontario Arts Council, Concordia University, the Department of Foreign Affairs, and Jean-François Somchynsky at the Canadian Embassy in Tokyo.

In thinking about blindness, I am indebted to the wit and scope of Jacques Derrida's *Memoirs of the Blind: The Self Portrait and Other Ruins,* first published in French as *Mémoirs d'aveugle: L' autoportrait et autres ruines* (Louvre in 1991), then translated and published by the University of Chicago Press, 1993. I owe the epigraph from Peter Greenaway's *The Draughtsman's Contract* to Pascale-Anne Brault and Michael Nass, who brought the comment to my attention in their Translators' Preface.

I have grown to believe that a really intelligent man makes an indifferent painter, for painting requires a certain blindness — a partial refusal to be aware of the options.

Peter Greenaway, *The Draughtsman's Contract*

. . . blindness is often the price to pay for anyone who must finally open some eyes, his own or another's, in order to recover sight or gain access to a spiritual light. The paradox stems from the fact that the blind man thus becomes the best witness, a chosen witness. In fact, a witness, as such, is always blind. Witnessing substitutes narrative for perception.

Jacques Derrida, *Memoirs of the Blind*

flying blind

FLYING BLIND

1. *Voyeur*

Can't help it, I have my eye
on John in East Jerusalem, the way
he folds his undershirts,

places papers neatly on a chest
of drawers. I watch, indecent,
as he explores the surfaces

we occupy, memorizes
distance, lays down latitudes
of privacy. Does the mirror

see John station himself
in front? No coy expressions
of self-love, only a man

shaving his face, soap driven
before the razor like a bow-wave.
I hang about as if he were

a ruin. His blindness unclothes
me, is an unreflecting pool.
Yesterday at Dar-El Tifl

orphanage he was a magnet,
children drawn to him
as to a fresh start,

the lame, the unloved
squinting ones, sensing an Eden
of possibility. A young girl

biting the nail of her little
finger to the quick tells him softly
in Arabic she is Lebanese.

Another dances while he plays
and sings. They don't stare
or share my fear of the blind,

the terrible blank gaze
that sees, a God's-eye,
everything there is

to see. Dark glasses
usher John's eyes to shadow,
his mask of blindness

makes me almost visible.
*This T-shirt, is it white
or blue?* he asks.

2. *The Best Samaritan*

Consider the dust. It lies
upon the tongue. Centuries
invested in a smile, olive trees
that bear the martyrs' names.

The High Priest smiles,
extends a hand in greeting.
Amram, who calls himself
a Palestinian Jew, speaks Arabic

to John, English to me, lives
in style (one could say
high style) on a mountaintop
in Nablus, ministers to a flock

of nine hundred Samaritans.
Twenty-six centuries
of documented habitation:
what do I know about pride

of place? And the intifada?
Yes, Amram explains, a building
was torched, but he phoned
Abu Amar in Tunis, was reimbursed

within days. Not so lucky
his Arab brothers, their demolished
houses lining the road uphill.
A few hours later John and I

will promenade among the ruins
of the Temple of Augustus
at Sebastiyeh, where the Baptist's
head was served on a platter,

where Omri, Ahab and Jeroboam
watched ivory palaces toppled
by invaders. Alexander the Great,
John Hyrcanus and Sargon II

the Assyrian had time to kill
and axes to grind in Samaria.
Against such history, L-5,
a herniated disc and my sciatic

nerve screaming blue murder.
The blind leading the lame.
Sacrificial blood stains Amram's
hands at Passover, fingers that caress

the ancient Scroll of Pentateuch
in Nablus dial the touch-tone
phone to distant Tunis.
A shepherd leads a dozen

goats along the ancient path.
His son, on foot, keeps strays
in line with a small stick,
the branch of an olive tree

for another branch of the family
claiming Abraham as father.
Bared throat, the sudden
intervention. I tried to call

home, could hear the phone
reverberate in empty
rooms. I wanted belief. No
blinding light, just something

that would endure partisan
struggles, shifts in power.
Dream on. The dead
donkey at the crossroads,

legs extending like ramrods
from the bloated carcass.
An army jeep stirs dust
not far from Jacob's Well,

where the Samaritan woman
asked for living water. I can feel
the stones recoil, hidden
springs cry out in disbelief

at road-blocks, guns, free passage
still denied. And clever diplomatic
Amram serves his coffee
black and sweet.

3. *Moses Among the Rushes*

I never intended to document
the lives of saints, their fingers warped
by continuous prayer, bodies
emitting an electromagnetic
glow. Disciples either, lugging
their pamphlets and self-
importance. Scanning the rushes,
I notice a stranger has co-opted
my face, my voice. I watch,
appalled, as this impostor

invades the small screen. Why
do Doug and his camera crew
not acknowledge the deception?
A small vehicle enters the frame,
backs out to a parking spot. Izzat
is telling of his solitary confinement.
My impersonator asks the writer
how he smuggled out his letters.
Izzat responds like a man who feels
all value disappear from the words

he speaks. He has plenty to lose
talking to foreigners, rendering fixed
and intractable the soft glottals
that cradle his narrative. I'm touched
again by these generous epistles
to literary mentors, including Israelis,
inscribed in a minute Arabic hand
on scraps of paper, rolled in cellophane
and passed from mouth to mouth by kiss
during family visits. Extraneous

background noise. My doppelganger
projects an irritating nasal voice
and nervous edge I might have fixed
with coaching. And Christ, he's used
that tasteless pun about kisses
with a subtext. John's lucky to be blind
in this instance. He gets an extra hour
of sleep and can replay his dream-script
while chalking up rest and REM-time
on the ravelled sleeve. The High 8,

on the other hand, is not blind enough,
relentlessly gathering detail,
knitting names, gestures and objects
into a fictional fabric not even the ruthless
guillotine of the film editor can rectify.
There in the cutting room I'll be
dubbed, patched, excised, superfluous
and unattractive pieces strewn underfoot,
a new creature emerging, a plastic
Frankenstein to call my own. Izzat

will have altered, too, his face
on film still ignorant of the wave
of pain set to engulf him fourteen days
after this interview, when settlers
on the rampage in a school in Ramallah
shoot and kill his son of seventeen.

So much for witness, prophecy.
The documents I smuggle out
on videocassette have aged as much
as they've distorted all I've seen.

4. *Flying Blind*

When the poet's blood
shifted hemispheres, streams
were in full flood, airports
buzzed, public statues
exposed themselves along

sunlit esplanades. Someone
in a Jerusalem suburb
was stockpiling weapons,
composing prayers. What
has this to do with a poet's

wintry demise, you rightly
inquire. Words modified again
in living guts? I have nothing
against the desert. That it is rock,
not sand, may be a matter

of remorse to certain clientele.
Not me. I'm pigging out
with John and Hisham
in a Bethlehem cafe.
Except for two blind Arabs

and a sighted minority
consuming chicken shish kebabs,
the place is empty. Smartly
dressed, Hisham has a Ph.D.
from the States and a job

waiting in Michigan.
Home briefly to refurbish
domestic relations. Four hands
scuttle across platters, up
the sides of glasses. Spiders,

bottom-feeders, anxious
to know what is there. We'd
disgraced ourselves at Bethlehem
University, leaving abruptly
after an hour of fake Platonic

dialogue we were told the study
of English helps adapt, think
critically, use technology, and work
in a multicultural setting. *Merde,*
I whispered to John, too loudly,

given the Vatican support this dump
gets, no wonder the paper's written
by someone named Pope. My visually
challenged friends have scoffed
most of the chicken, ordered seconds

of bread which they eat unbuttered
in the Arab fashion. Hisham,
fastidious, pays his share, makes
connections at Deheishe, the refugee
camp where he stays with his parents

and equally blind brother. They
owe their condition to vitamin
deficiency, contaminated water.
Ahmad offers a typical account
of military abuse. I'm mesmerized

not by the story but the absolute
stillness of the teller, no light
emanating from his dead eyes.
If the animus is not visible
there, where does it hang

out — in these nosy, brash,
interrogating hands? Without
benefit of higher education or
the gospel according to Carol Pope,
Ahmad relates how urine,

excrement and blood
mingled freely in the cell,
where he could neither stand
nor lie down, how they
punched him in the kidneys

as he clung to the jeep.
A crash course. He
calls it the central experience
of his life. Prison gave meaning,
purpose, made him

part of the intifada. I think
of the two Israeli hikers
killed this week in Wadi Kelt,
throats opened. Yeats gone,
his rough beast too close

to Bethlehem for comfort.
And John so overcome
he has to leave the room.
The brothers wave as our car
descends the open-sewer

dirt track into Bethlehem
proper. O little town,
mute and doggo like language
itself before the spectre
of a twenty-first century.

5. *Luck of the Irish*

A day off from politics,
though my back's killing me.
No polluted villages, jailhouse
confessions. West Jerusalem
shops. And, with luck, hot
dogs, a couple of beers,

an ice cream cone. Thermal
yin-yang. My favourite
outing as a kid in Vancouver
was a trip to the dairy.
For a dime you got a huge
scoop of Arctic Ice Cream

or half a brick for twenty-five
cents. As the cooling flavours
teased my throat and made
my forehead ache, Larry Flynn
was organizing shipments
in the warehouse out back.

I'd turned seven, my mother
was dying but I did not know it
yet, and life seemed good.
My health was okay. I weighed
sixty-seven pounds, Larry's
exact weight at twice my age

when transferred to Lager IV.
Die Fir Lager, "the hospital,"
specialized in helping the sick
and handicapped shuffle off
their mortal coils. Malingerers
were infected with typhus

and rallied to join the no longer
marching saints piled high
in adjoining sheds. To find
his brother, Larry ran
from shed to shed shifting
corpses whose skin, stretched

tight as Easy-Wrap, had a
translucent hue. In response
to his calls and frantic
rummaging, an arm rose
from among the doomed,
rocked slowly back

and forth, a pale flower
or metronome, saying,
Wait, 78850, I am not yet
dead. Instead of fighting
in Palestine, Larry began
a second life in Vancouver

feeding ovens in an Italian
bakery, scrubbing the killing
floor of the Alberta Meat Market,
sections for hanging, scalding,
eviscerating, chilling, cutting
and processing. He graduated

to grinding organs and guts
for fertilizers, dogfood. As I weigh
the relative merits of twenty
flavours, Larry is in the freezer
backstage at Arctic Ice Cream
arguing with his brother and friends

in management about the ethics
of changing his name from Freeman
to Flynn. He toys with a flashlight
in the dim interior of the vault,
cupping the beam in his palm,
watching the warm blood pulse

and circulate. I couldn't take
my eyes off him as he gave
his testimony to a propaganda
workshop at the art gallery
on Robson Street, twelve teenagers
intent on his body language,

apologetic tone, the amount
of water he consumed, surviving
again the ordeal that will not
be denied. Our place of meeting
was a courtroom in its previous
incarnation, raised platform,

dark wood panels still intact.
As I finish my maple-walnut
cone, a trade mission from Japan
mounts the cobbled West Jerusalem
street. Male dancers and kimonoed
women distribute glossy leaflets

in English and Hebrew. I recall
my wife's delight on discovering
the manufacturer's label
on some lingerie from Asia:
WOMEN SWEAR. I wrote a letter
from my office in the barn

trying to explain my position,
conscious of her sitting fifty
feet away in the house, reading
manuscripts. What's the point,
trying to ascribe blame? she asked.
It's over. She was wearing

the blue and white striped
kimono we'd bought at a hotel
in Tokyo, the words KIMI
RYOKAN in capital letters
on the lapel. I still loved her.
My desk occupied the contested

area between two box stalls
where Simon the appaloosa
and Chadwick the baseball donkey
had jostled for space and for hay
under the old dispensation.
Predetermined banalities —

ice cream and evil. His bray
began as an asthmatic wheeze
and grew to such proportions
the horse used to quit the barn
at a gallop. A vacuum cleaner
with hiccups. Exhausted

by his performance, he'd lean
against the partition for support.
A hand rises from the judicial bench
to guide us. Or conduct our requiem.
If Mengele jerks his thumb towards
the bathhouse, we'll be saved.

6. *Eyeless in Gaza*

Late night TV documentary
on the military occupation.
This time a personality profile
of the commanding officer.
Young, tough, presented
as someone who wants peace,
if only to get out of this hellhole
and back to Jerusalem, Tel Aviv.
No mention of Palestinians,

the 10,489 injured or dead
in Gaza in the early stages
of the intifada. Creative
bookkeeping. No budding
humanist, a career soldier
determined to keep the lid on,
suppress revolt. His outpost
commands the city, binoculars
picking up every movement

in the streets, down to the infrequent
shitting of donkeys. He keeps an eye
on equipment, the gravel-sprayer
first used on women in 1988
during a demonstration in Nablus,
and an eye on Dr. Eyed el-Sarraj
in the only medical clinic. He condones
the kidnapping of victims of military
violence to intimidate families

and destroy evidence. Tradition,
part of the great chain of command
that reaches back to Menachem Begin
who blew up a Jerusalem hotel,
killing a hundred people. State
terrorism. Turn territories
into suburbs, reduce Palestinian
nationalism to a municipal matter
regulated by ethnic councils,

folklore clubs, cultural grants. Want
to publish a book of radical poets?
Why not? Remember to acknowledge
your patrons on the copyright page.
A summer job in repertory
in Haifa restoring the wings
of angels, where they hung like albino
bats along the south wall
of the props department. Edeet,

who smiled at his awkwardness
and thought he had promise as an actor,
left for the States after 1982
when 400,000 took to the streets
in horror at Sabra and Shatilla
and nothing changed. Annexation
carried obligations (citizenship,
suffrage, the usual abstractions),
but *autonomy*, ambivalent,

permitted settlement and gradual
displacement of the local population.
He's read the reports, including
those perpetrated by P.H.R.I.C.
and S.C.F. Better written
and at least as credible. Rami Abu
Samra, 10, shot in the head at the door
of the Sala Eddin mosque, where
he replenished the water supply

in the refrigerator, tended the garden
(the I.D.F. claimed he had thrown,
or aided in throwing, a petrol bomb).
Manal Samour, 14, shot in the chest
at Shatti Refugee Camp, not for stones
thrown, but for helping a friend
injured in the same melee. Hanada Abu
Sultan, shot in the head entering
a pharmacy with her sister, ferried

to Shifa' Hospital, then Tel Hashomer
and a hurried, improvised funeral
attended by only ten relatives.
They'd be driving Mercedes by now
if they'd let us get on with the inevitable
expansion. Volkswagens, anyway.
They carry politics like disease.
Dogs licking wounds. Simcha
was wrong: there's nothing

clean about a dog's mouth. Maggots
are more efficient against infection.
What's heavier than a mother's empty
arms? You can shove those cameras
up your ass. Liberals, Sunday School
teachers. We'd be rotting still in Dachau
if we'd waited for you. *For every Jew*
that dies another angel mounts the wind,
its precious eyebrows lines of dancing fire.

Editor's Note
P.H.R.I.C.: Palestinian Human Rights Information Centre.
S.C.F.: Save the Children Fund.
I.D.F.: Israeli Defence Force.

Of course, none of this is reliable, not even the poetic flourish
at the end, designed, perhaps, to draw attention away from
other more blatant biases in the text. What the television crews
"orchestrated" — or "cooked", as we used to say in science class
— has prompted from the author an equally distorted picture.
As reader, you have to wonder what the governing mythos is in
this kind of writing, and what this sort of deliberate blindness
can possibly hope to achieve. This entry, if you haven't already
noticed, is written from an omniscient point of view, a nameless,
unidentifiable narrator purporting access to the mind of the
televized version of a military commander, whose spatial and
temporal circumstances are so remote as to be essentially
unknowable.

There is an overabundance of angels and eyes (despite the title) in this text, implying special pleading or privileging of the divine and the empirical. An eye for an eye, a stone for a stone, and that dubious category, the eye-witness. All things considered, you can't help but suspect the author, if not of outright anti-Semitism (and this for Arabs as well as Jews, both being Semitic peoples), at least of general misanthropy, perhaps attributable to an unfortunate self-hatred induced in childhood. Too long a victim himself, he now resorts to the tyranny of words to victimize others and distort reality, appropriating stories to achieve authenticity, marshalling so-called first-hand experiences in quaint personal anecdotes and sly narratives and passing them off as evidence, which any reliable historiographer will tell you is always constructed.

7. Buying Time

Okay, so I'm the one who's
blind, imposing my own reading
of events, of John. I close

my eyes to what I can't
accommodate. Theodor Herzl
had the same problem

during ten days in Palestine
in 1898. He noticed no Arabs,
only a *mixed multitude*

of beggars lining a dusty road
to observe the Kaiser's visit.
Unless he was a certifiable

villain, Herzl's blindness
was necessary to the Jewish-
Ottoman Land Company

he was trying to promote.
Meeting with Abdul Hamid
in Istanbul in 1902 to propose

his scheme for colonization,
he lied to the Sultan, pretending
friendship and offering to solve

the problem of Turkish debt.
Meanwhile Ibrahim, Grand
Master of Ceremonies, put

his own spin on events,
and Izzet al-Abed, a Syrian
serving as court chamberlain,

used his poker-face
and diplomatic skills to full
advantage, buying time,

imposing restrictions, faking
outrage. Back at the hotel,
after he'd declared

in a farewell letter his people's
*respect and love for the august
person of the Caliph,*

*the only great friend we have
on earth,* Herzl sat down
to his diary and described

his hosts as *bums, a tangle
of venomous snakes,*
their leader *shabby*

and *noxious*, with big ears
and the *hooked nose
of a Punchinello.* Duplicity

protects us, writes Paul de Man,
accused of collaborating
with the Nazis, his eloquent

pen traversing the page
in the service of a formidable
intellect, an unnameable past.

Rhetoric transgresses, why
should this text be different,
my own narrative a nest

of delusions. The population
of Jews in Palestine
less than two percent in 1900,

de Rothschild's support
notwithstanding. I was searching
for something incorruptible

to translate, how we come
to depend on love, the myriad
little gestures so often

taken for granted, the way
a wrist bends and the hand
opens towards you, lines

fully exposed. Home plate.
Was first base even an option?
Hit the ball, then try to stay

mounted as they push-pull
the rude beast around the infield.
Lips move silently,

trying out the words. I keep
thinking, if redemption's
your game, travel by donkey.

8. Borderline Schizophrenics

What am I doing in this rented vehicle, driving John to the Lebanese border? I could be interviewing Hamas or meeting dissident Jews in Tel Aviv. Instead, I'm chauffeur to a Homeric Arab napping in the seat beside me, more at ease in his dim world than I in my troubled visible one. Yesterday we visited a hospital in East Jerusalem whose funding was cut as a result of unwise alignments in the Gulf War. Minutes into our interview, the presiding doctor excuses himself and returns with a peasant from Gaza, whose son needs immediate medical attention. The first procedure, diagnostic, is to be done by Israelis since they have the best equipment. Given positive results, treatment can begin. The bald challenge works and we part with the desired cash in travellers' cheques. The old man thanks Allah, the doctor thanks us, and we thank Nawal Halawa for setting us up. The sick child, who wants only to go home with his family to Gaza, runs screaming down the corridor when he hears the good news. The cost of playing God is modest here. Even a Jew like Bill Freedman from Chicago, who teaches poetry at Haifa University, has to moonlight to make ends meet. He's a paid shrink in the evenings, composes poems and dreams of spending a sabbatical with his girlfriend in Montreal, earning twice as much and teaching half the hours. Metaphysician heal thyself. John is unemployed back home, though doctored, published and a gifted teacher. The prejudice has as much to do with blindness as race. Here such stigmas don't exist. John's basking not only in adulation but in two job offers, which he can't accept because of danger to wife and kids. The redemptive power of work. Bronwen, five, seeing me spend so much time at home filling blank pages with words, said, Dad, what are you going to be when you grow up? *Touché!* Maybe I'll be a soldier or a singer, an engineer or television comic. Wake up, Farouk, we're at the border, in more ways than one. Poets arise! Let trumpets sound! We'll march triumphant through the ruins of Jericho, Beirut. Twenty-two years in exile. John breathes the familiar coastal air, thrusts his arms between the iron bars of the barrier so his hands, at least, are back home in Lebanon, the same ten fingers that picked up a shiny metallic device dropped by jet-fighters in a field outside his village, manna from Israel that put the sun and stars to sleep. *G'day, mates.* The blond Jewish soldier from Adelaide sweats out the noon shift. An Uzi, a cup of Coke in styrofoam.

9. *A Night at the Jerusalem Hotel*

A night of beer and singing
in the restaurant garden, tables set
under a canopy of vines
and creepers. John navigates
the cobbled path, the cane
with its white rubber tip

nosing flowerbeds. He settles
into a rattan chair, striped
watermelon shape of the lute
on his knees. We're waiting
for George, Musa and Nader,
our principle singers and revellers.

Maxine Kaufmann expected too,
with friends from *The Other Israel.*
She protests internments, illegal
expropriations, writes articles
about Yesh Gvul, soldiers
who refuse to serve in West Bank

or Gaza. This week Maxine's
interviewing Bedouins
displaced from traditional
grazing lands in the Negev desert.
Our local friends all graduates
of the jails and intifada. Loahez,

tortured and imprisoned at fifteen
for joining a group that promoted
Palestinian rights. Musa, hairdresser
and cut-up, who mocks nationalist
lyrics, refuses to speak of prison.
And George, a high school teacher

who loves poetry and spends evenings
with his girlfriend in the padded
cells of the music department
at Hebrew University, practising scales
on the beloved's vertebrae, scoring
intricate sonatas. Nader dreamed

of engineering but his father's
death intervened. He put
his ambitions on hold and ran
the offset press in his mother's
basement. Before the ink dried
he was jailed. Lights go on

along the walls of the Old City.
At the depot next door buses
have bedded down awaiting
the Messiah. Our guests
have come and John is tuning up
— we'll be transported yet.

10. *An Eye for the Ladies*

There's a legend in my family about a pianist
born blind somewhere in Glasgow
or Edinburgh. It was classical, I recall (his repertoire,
that is), but I prefer to think

he played at some small pub in Lanarkshire,
chords and melodies filtered through smoke
and small talk, that he had a glass of beer
on the ledge above his keyboard, beside a rose

the management provided, or an old lover.
As evening progressed his face would shine
like Stevie Wonder's. He'd lean into the fragrance
of that rose and remember the sweet funk

of sex, the flowery combat of nerve endings
on fire. A reasonable fantasy even
for Presbyterians. After all, they named
their greatest poet Burns. Women, of course,

all love him, no snap judgements or false
assumptions based on appearance to sour
or complicate relations. Perhaps he smells
their heat as animals do, or hears the lonely echo

behind a voice, substrata of desire. Fingers
that caress ivory might also coax music
from tired flesh. Describe yourself, he'd say,
your skin's as soft as feathers and words

that take flight from your lips nest lovingly
in my ear. Women who can't let go, abandon
notions of performance and feel their bodies
unfurl, all the Anne Gregorys once comforted

by Yeats for the odds against yellow hair
finding true love. When I mention these
fantasies to John on the road to Nazareth,
before we offer a ride to two Israeli soldiers

returning from sentry duty at the Lebanese border,
he shakes with laughter, then tells me about
the woman who picked him up in Montreal
when he was twenty and the two Arabs, seated

behind him on the bus, sick with jealousy and cursing
the injustice of such beauty wasted on the blind.
They never knew he understood their conversation
until he smiled and said goodbye in Arabic.

11. *In which I assume, recklessly, the mantle of Augustine*

This, for the record, is my
last confession. I call it quits,
bequeath to Francis and his
feathered friends my quill,

my quiddity, my *quid pro quo.*
Eyes tempted still by the world
and its forms. Corporeal light
distorts, its dangerous sweetness

makes me colour-drunk; and
paintings, Lord, bold, concupiscent
in their revelation, hymn me
from devotions. Isaac, old, blind,

bestows his blessing on the wrong
son, dressed in goatskins
to simulate his hairy brother
Esau. Then Jacob in his turn

preferring Ephraim, signals
crossed, but doing, so we're told,
your will. Too much beauty
immolates, corrupts both viewer

and viewed. Sacrifice of
sight allows me to transcend
the merely visible. The quietist
weighs anchor, the anchorite

sets sail. Blind man's bluff's
a game for those in love
with shadows. The blindfold
executes its will, real

wool pulled over imaginary
peepers. The blind navigator
burns his charts and sails, oblivious,
in an opaque glass sphere.

12. Horsefly

Leghorn Joshua stands in judgement over jerichoed walls, breast a juggernaut, revving his reveille, brassy orchestrations love-juicing the warm eggs. He pipes a slack-ass sun over the unscrubbed, unknit brow of earth. Dew-drenched, the birthed barn inches, solemn, dayward; its animal-freight shifts and groans, lugged organs of delight. Yes yes to horse-heart, consuming its straggle-beard of hay in doorway, and the baleful doppelganger donkey in dismal disarray, shadowing in shirtsleeves. Swallows swoop from perch to pitchfork, perfect plagiarists glimpsing the death of song. Mouse glides, subversive, through the privileged motes, banks on absence. And I, fly-by-night, thank you O God — even as I languish in bird-beak, ontological stupor — for the undigested grain in horse shit, the sweet blood shed nightly in your honour.

aggregate resources

MINUS 20

The stove is damped so air constricted
whistles in the draft and metal casings creak
as they expand. Jays impatient and aggressive
at the feeder. Me, too, I'm on survival mode,

consume more carbohydrates than I need.
My body, slow, impolitic, resists
the old imperatives. I'll ski the back trail
yet, if temperatures permit. The crippled

cedars, permanently bent from wrapping
round a fallen maple as they grew, now
form a bold menorah that lights my spirit
as I pass. Meanwhile the cold dictates,

decrees this lethargy, this slow combustion
holding back an ice age in the blood.

THE QUALITY OF LIGHT

The quality of light is what arrests the man
moving, by gradations, through the snowy field
on skis. He eyes the outlines of trail broken yesterday,
shaped and contoured by wind, wind that never
sleeps yet seldom tires of letting its cold tongue

sculpt and sweep a tentative world of forms.
Two steps behind, conserving energy by keeping
to the beaten track, the dog takes bites of snow
and contemplates an archeology of smell:
spoors, markings of its undomesticated kind

that cross this man-made path at random,
making their own incursions in the narrative.
As the sun's rays, denied by angle and position
of the earth their customary part, ricochet
a thousand times among the mirrored crystals,

emerging more intense than light itself, so the man
stumbles from thought to thought, a blinking
new born Lazarus. Sculpted troughs, too narrow
now for use, bind together harnesses, or nudge
one tip across another for a fall. The dog looks on,

one could say amused, though not itself sure-footed
on this stage. Man and dog recall how February
storms cause dunes of snow to curl like breaking
waves. Imagine them explorers in Sahara, grit
of sand in mouth, eyes asquint against abrasion.

Flesh dreams water, requires protection from sun
that burns whatever peeks from hair or cloth. Light
there is thick and granular and radiates in ridges
from the ground. Here, the man with bamboo poles
extending from his arms learns to cover space

by watching his companion, reaching back in time
to when four limbs propelled him. The rigid sticks
beneath his feet are unconverging lines in a parallel
universe of cold, where he pauses, almost snowblind,
old, and thinks of history every day rewritten,

revisionist monks, amnesiac ideologues in flowing
robes. He sees them near stone fences fast at work,
pretends scant notice and, ploughing his way
through a no-man's-land of ice, records
the wins and losses on both sides.

HIGH GROUND

Submerged beneath three feet of snow
my neighbour's boat serves notice
of an option set aside. He's not a neighbour,
not exactly, owns but does not live

on fifty acres severed from the parcel
that contained my land. He planned
a house for his retirement, the baleful boat
an emerald to adorn his fantasy. It sits

on high ground near the unused sugar shack,
host to small animals inscribed with memories
of a flood, an inland ocean lapping struts
and ribs. They winter déclassé this scuttled

ark. The trailer rusts, the mast has grown
a beard of moss. Receding waters took their time
to carve the fossils in my patio, unlike
the splitting fibreglass near Archie's keel.

IF

If, when bright bedraggled creatures
light on branches of the hybrid poplar
like so many Christmas decorations
and mimic the fabric birds you sagely

purchased; if, when the old logs pitch
and groan at night as heat withdraws
and make like sly intruders on the stairs
so you too lie awake remembering

the axe; if, when the cupboard door
blows open during an easterly
and the ghosts of unused kitchenware
peer sadly from behind the stack

of sixty-watt bulbs; if, when the traps
are empty but unsprung, the snacks
of medium cheddar and peanut butter
lifted with no trace but the telltale

droppings; if, when the fridge hums
its anthem to icy artifice and the old
blast furnace farts its turgid tropic
symphony in three-four time, well . . .

INCHING PAST THE EIGG ROAD IN A STORM

I leave the late train in Alexandria,
travel the twelve miles home
by car. Wind from the east causes
drifts to form, so severe my lane

disappears in places. A huge bank
looms above me like the white whale
poised above the *Pequod*. Loose snow,
hypnotic, races back and forth

across the surface as if it can't
make up its mind. My time capsule
plunges into ridge after ghostly
ridge, shudders but holds the road.

Luckily, there's not another car
in sight. I relax at the helm.
My highbeams, sealed and fortified,
scan the stretch from Fassifern

to Laggan. Rivière Rigaud,
its assets frozen, its testimony
unconvincing. I can tell the log houses
are still alive by small puffs

of smoke exhaled from chimneys.
The moon's reflected light reflects
again off snow, so barns and silos
might be markers in a gale.

GROUSE

Each day the grouse explodes
at a certain juncture in the cedars,
beating a quick departure
through the lower branches.

If I forget, the sudden movement
startles me; more often, though,
I hold my breath and try to guess
the exact spot, exact moment

of lift-off. Experience tells me
there's a nest nearby, the frantic
exit just a ploy to put me off
the track; the hound, too, whose

shortcut intersects the perilous
flight path of the grouse. I know
the dolour of the empty nest. My mother,
half a century dead, pushes north

along Commercial Drive a pram,
faces a mountain bearing the name
of the bird my passage has dislodged,
smiles at the mewling infant self

I can't imagine. My father, startled,
beats his own retreat in wartime,
drums for wings. Distraction
works as well as lethal talons

if the intruder proves disinterested,
inept. A scent has caught the dog's
attention. As for me, I read the signs,
briefly pause to urinate, push on.

AGGREGATE RESOURCES

We quarry down towards the heat, the molten
core, part of a cool circumference that wishes —
what? — to be transfigured. These heretic cells,
like Joan's, inch towards flame, oblivion.

It was warm in the womb but treacherous,
those waters that expelled us not to be
trusted. We huddled in cities, malls, cafés,
our electric fires simulating paradise.

Something fallen from the sky — they did not
need newspaper records to confirm it —
shivered, finding itself, to use the vernacular,
out in the cold. No way back, the damaged

wings folded neatly, stored in the hollow
of an old maple. We knuckled down,
abandoned metaphor, split rocks, part
of the chain gang, a link or two below

where we deserved. But what has merit
to do with it? *Darkly wise but rudely great*
pretty well summed it up. Apple blossoms
that first spring, I admit, surprised us.

If you listened carefully you could hear
the grass grow. *Ng,* it said, *ng.* We learned
to sweat, a breakthrough of sorts. Parts
of kill festooned on makeshift platters

rewarded hawk and hound. Antiquated
usage, easy to document. Bugle
calls, the dead in neat rows. A large buck
grazes upwind. Cedars, unstable in

thin soil, topple: small kingdoms. The hanging
man who had, it seems, even as quarry,
a sense of humour, punned on a disciple's
name, claiming the rock sufficient ground

on which to build. Who says this slab, this
ragged shield, is not enough to build
consensus on? It would give that preposterous
Greek, already weak-heeled, flat feet.

Stones polished, sucked; all the heresies
you can muster, placed on mantels, windowsills.
Cornerstones. Was it a covering of snow,
plain as yogurt, prompted this meditation

on desire? *Morphophily:* the tribal history
of human forms, so crazy on the tongue
you overlook the pedantry. We're
signed, let's agree, for the duration,

this exposed crust, cooled to granite. Cain,
be damned. Tropics, too. *Quelques arpents
de neige.* A royal write-off. Words, bedrock.
Such redemption as there is begins here.

WATERMARKS

Why do the oldest wounds ache so?
On the trail today I found two bloodstains
in the snow. Not piss, but the pale rose
shade of blood absorbed and diffused

by snow crystals. There were no prints
discernible nearby. Some small bird
or rodent, like the vole my shovelling
disturbed, exposed to celestial scrutiny,

snatched up into the cold sky. Not even
bodily translated like Elijah or the prophet
Mohammed, rising from the dome of the rock
on his vertical-take-off stallion. For such

creatures, the delicate, tentative ones
whose phone numbers you should have recorded
in pencil, the ground closes its fist in a stark
refusal of seed. The red-tailed hawk

Jan startled when she brought in wood
kills without compunction living things
for whom there is no amnesty. Partial
thaw has turned the fields to a vast crust of ice

back to the roseate treeline. Tops of trees,
tinted by a declining sun, turn mauve
before they disappear. Shadow puppets,
lines of ink on good bond paper, acid-free.

little sleeps

HOMEWORK

As I turn the car up the driveway,
I can see Jan in the rear-view mirror
dragging Mac and the four cats, all dead,
on a toboggan over the hill to the first field.

We couldn't bear to see him suffer a winter
of isolation in the barn as rabies
sowed havoc in his blood, this haywire
border collie whose speed carried him

up the trunk of the maple, where he'd bite
the first branch and drop eight feet
to the ground, the breed too high-strung
for easy domesticity or the safety

of small children. I held him in my arms
while the vet injected a fatal solution into his veins.
A slight quiver as the heart and other organs
registered shock and he was gone,

all that neurotic energy reduced to mere weight
and the damp nose going dry as I chalked up
another F as caregiver. I roll the window
down to wave, but Jan doesn't notice, her body

bent to the terrible task, chipping away
at the frozen ground with the new spade
from Canadian Tire. I recheck my briefcase
and the bundle of unmarked essays

on the back seat, depress the accelerator,
and ease gas into the humming cylinders.
Wheels spin in the loose gravel, then the car
leaps forward onto the paved road.

R.B.I.

The young racoon nets a low-flying bat
outside my window. Unperturbed by the light
or her human audience, she scoops the night flyer
from the air with the deftness of a shortstop

snagging a line drive just beyond the reach
of the third baseman. I feel strangely honoured
by the spectacle of this prowler, no doubt wintering
in my barn among bales of old hay. She steals

more than bases while I sleep. At certain moments
in the night she is inches from my face,
this mask of repose behind which cells riot
and restore themselves, archetypes battle it out

in cranial videos, and electrical impulses
signal the animal presence. *Bienvenue*, I say,
in case she's not bilingual, remembering
Thelma's story of how racoons like to wash

their food before eating it and how this rookie,
having filched a discarded bag of crackers
from the garbage, looked so baffled beside the pond
as they melted one by one in her delicate hands.

CHRISTENE'S POEM

Before fog lifted and the last of the pack-ice
cleared the harbour, Commander
Hodgson's carrots had grown a full inch
in the warm confines of the greenhouse,
locals already muttering
about the rich man's foibles,
scandal of pulling carrots prematurely —
no longer than a baby finger! — when
there's hunger about and growing things
should reach their term;

what she wouldn't tell that man, given
half a chance, until the day
Mrs. Hodgson invited the women
of Jersey Cove to tea, a dozen of them
in Sunday best, delivered by boat,
delicate china on their laps,
sugar spoons small enough
to feed an infant with,
and unable to speak
above a whisper, or make
more than the most rudimentary
replies, women who gutted cod and tuna,
stoked fires, whose exhausted bones
performed the work of barometers, who pushed life
out into the fiery air only to snatch it back,
bit by bit, from the terrible teeth
of the sea, winding
their dead in strips of inferior cotton:

a gifted boy, escaping coal pits
only to disappear off-shore, mining
the emerald deeps, blue limbs
not yet mature, locked in a slow dance
with drifting kelp, fish scales
clinging to his curly hair
like confetti.

DANCES WITH COYOTES

The black driver, who tells me
he once stopped over in Labrador
with the U.S. Army
during the war, turns up
the radio for the national news.

A man in California
has killed one of his two wives
in order to avoid a conviction
for bigamy; an arsonist
claims he torched
twelve churches in Florida
because they were using computers
that stimulated his homosexual desires.

They promised I'd find a woman
behind every tree in Iceland.
The driver pauses to glance at me
in the rear-view mirror
as we merge with the freeway
heading north to *La Cañada*
(nothing to do with home,
the word is Spanish for *canyon*).

In an hour I'll be driving
past expensive houses, the industry's
rising stars, dissipated comets.

Alchemy: translate the self's
arid suburbs into dollars. Our host
will have had a truckload of fresh snow
dumped in his front yard to simulate
a northern Christmas, neighbour kids sliding
and the family dog leaping several feet
to catch the hard-packed balls
of snow.

I want to ask about Rodney King
and the aftermath of the riots
in South L.A., war zone
of the disinherited, but the moment
passes as we enter foothills
where coyotes serenade after dark
and feed on the plump bodies
of domestic animals.

The driver flashes me a grin
as he wheels the green minivan
onto the exit ramp. *Yes, sir,*
a woman behind every tree;
but weren't no trees,
not one.

RWANDA HILTON

A spectral daughter,
anchored only by her will
and fragile grasp. A son

whose bloat and fevered eyes
belie the word *relief*.
The mother, in her madness,

tries to sell a pair of pumps
with pink silk uppers. They stand
erect on a scrap of cloth

on high ground, awaiting
the return of Fashion who will
step forward from among

the clusters of the dying, slip
her small black delicate Cinderella
feet into place, and the whole

nightmare will miraculously be over.
With light hearts the dead
settle into new lives, exacting

no payment in kind. Grieving
mothers imagine a heaven
depicted in *Elle* where clothes

eclipse food as the focus of desire,
where no one is angry or sick
or bleeds. Perfumed cesspools,

philanthropic bacteria. *Mais,*
à ce moment, mes amis, there are
no takers. Pink silk heels

command the cameraman's
attention and mine,
flanked by pieces of cheap

cutlery, as if the main course
on a table spread for one, saying:
Eat me, I'm beautiful!

TUAN JIM AT CORCOVADO

In the destructive element immerse.
Joseph Conrad, *Lord Jim*

I can't forget Stein's words, the noisy intake
of air, slurred gutterals. Sweat stood out
on his neck despite a faint breeze
that stirred the rattan. A reclining Buddha
with cigar and gin. The world is big enough

to lose myself, I thought. On the way up
I haggle with the driver. No, I don't want
the three-hour tour for fifty bucks,
not even the standard version for twenty.
I hand him twelve dollars, a third of the trip

to do on foot. He berates me as a cheapskate,
though I could have made a return visit
to Christ by funicular for half that amount.
After my climb fog begins to roll in and
I catch only the briefest glimpse of the beach

at Ipanema and the outstretched arms
of the saviour above me, blindly ploughing
mist like the blunt prow of the *Patna*.
Serves me right, haggling at the feet of Christ
for what — peanuts! Meanwhile, inexorable,

insensate, the ship drives on, engines
pulsing, surge of power turning the shaft and
cloverleaf of brass. A brutal trinity, stirring again
these atoms of desire. What propels me,
once-bitten, to seek in motion meaning, absolution?

Below, the jails are full, forests in flame,
the innocents equipped with switchblades,
guns. Innocents? I can't escape the old rhetoric
— crazy, I know — the notion it's all
redeemable, that a single gesture links me

to this stone face blessing inclement weathers.
If I could accept Stein's advice, considered,
avuncular, things might proceed, as he says
in his quaint accent, *swimmingly*. The waiter
brings a plate of tropical fruit and tea.

No hassle this time, prices on the frayed menu
fixed. The greenest bird, a *picaflor*,
draws nectar from red flowers hanging by my table.
Their name in Portuguese is *brinca
de princesa*, earrings of the princess.

TIDE TABLES

Grandma Carrie begs for water
but can't swallow. The tip of her tongue
probes the meniscus of clear liquid,

parched shoreline of lip.
Her body, once robust, melts
back to its elements.

I have nothing to give Sarcy,
she sobs, as my four-year-old clambers
up beside her on the floral

bedspread, radiant with well-being.
I never saw my grandmother
alive again or forgot that moment

and its equivocations. End-zones
between which I still stagger.
Active Pass. Tidal waters course

the narrow channel, as grains
of sand pelt through the hourglass
gap. Concern's a gift, a site

of transcendence. Back home,
blond curls lighting up her face,
my daughter asks if I believe in God

and heaven. I don't know for sure
about such things, I say, what do you
think? *When you die your bones*

go to the museum and your thoughts
go up into the sky like a balloon. Then she
laughs, resplendent on a bank of pillow.

THE TRIBE
for Margaret Laurence

Your voice on the car radio, the long slow
curves from Rupert to Hazelton.
A salmon-charged Skeena surges
past talus slopes, precipitous moraines.

You were talking to someone on the CBC
about — what else? — the tribe, taking
dominion, bringing our experience
of the land under imaginative control.

I watched headlights sweep from rockface
to nothingness as this same land fell away
and the valley yawed into drumming
silence. I knew by then about the tribe,

years since you cornered me in the kitchen
at Elm Cottage and said with finality,
Don't waste my time if you're not serious.
I marvel at the words. We were writers,

not lovers, yet you demanded a pledge.
Scary stuff for a poet with little to show,
who hadn't read Rilke. Your hooded eyes
reached back farther than Scotland, a deep

spring of wisdom in the Asian steppes. I'd
half-led half-carried you from your office
at Massey College to the seminar, your nerves
frazzled from a morning in divorce court

and my students awaiting the word, the decree
absolute. Years later, in Lakefield, you read me
Piper Gunn's lament in the broadest Scots,
an accent we could not shake off. And I wept

for you, myself, Piper Gunn, and all the lost
tribe of scribblers spinning their gossamer
filaments over the indecent vastness
of this land. And when copper divining rods

dipped in my hands in the groundskeeper's
house at Avebury, I thought of you, how
your voice transported me among the totems
at Hazelton, through so many dark nights,

out of the restrictive net of self-interest
and into the swirling waters, where scarred
beleaguered salmon exchange beauty for utility
in the flesh-destroying, blood-red urge to spawn.

POSTCARD FROM DUCK LAKE

There are no ducks at Duck Lake
when I arrive in late June,
the station wagon loaded down
with books and plants, two bicycles strapped
to the roof, wheels turning slowly
in wind off the reserve.

I think of Almighty Voice, facing
Middleton's cannon, then his own demons
in Duck Lake prison, a log and sod hut no bigger
than our last bedroom. Events large enough
to take the words out of his mouth.

I am moving house again, heading east
into Quebec's disputed territories,
only the still small voice of poetry
at my disposal. Not conscious
of treaty talks ahead, lying in bed
on Greene Avenue, infidelities spread out
on the patchwork quilt.
Peace talks? Not quite. Years
of sniping, guerrilla war,
embargoes. In Ottawa the plants
wither and die overnight
in the unventilated car.

Husbandry . . .

I lift my voice unto the hills
and hear the absence
echo.

DU FU AT CHESTNUT STATION

Waxing crescent moon freighted
with desire, birds taking respite in cedar branches
en route to southern

prefectures. And the poet,
savings exhausted, the gift of shallots
and yams already forgotten,

pauses to write a verse about his ailing horse,
his empty purse and a gatherer of acorns.
He records what is on his mind

with gaps large enough for a family
to fall through. He came to acquire property,
a rash gesture of welcome over wine,

as if a rugged vista offered better
prospects. Confessing complicity in the unjust
banishment of a friend at court, he blames

his wife and children for the inclement
weather and dire circumstances of this mountain
retreat. His monstrous reflection shatters the waters

of Dragon Pool. He recalls distant brothers, ponders
the final placement of his bones. Sick horse,
hungry eye, extravagant desire.

LITTLE SLEEPS

A weekend with the Wallace-Crabbes
near Separation Creek. Long walks
on the fragmented layers of rock
extending into waters
of the South Coast. Sectional slabs,
edges raised like stained glass
leading. Blowouts, a sandstone nut
dissolved or knocked out
by the action of waves, leaving a small
cavity of water, plants,
other organisms.

I bathe in accents, vocabulary,
post-colonial puns. In order
to pick up his sheila,
studying late, Jerzy found
a posi at the uni. Later, married,
he said, stepping out of the dunny:
Fair dinkum chook, what chance you got
with a larrikin like me?

The great fire consumed
much of the forest but leapt
over a single cottage
on the shore-line. Pain here,
a burning deep into moss and roots
I want to touch. Accretions of word and act
we cannot, in ourselves, forgive.
The weather in each face:
squalls, sunbursts,

fast-moving cloud. Academia,
soccer, arts administration,
skateboards, the dog's foot infected.

The search for yabbies
in a small pond in the Otways.
Chris, Marianne and the boys baiting string
with strips of old beef. A kangaroo
departs silent as a deer.

When I got the blue-lines back
from my Italian publisher, Chris says,
I found he had translated the word
nappies as little sleeps.

CIRCULAR QUAY

Young Chinese at water's edge,
playing a horse-head fiddle.

Notes from the classical repertoire
curl around my thoughts
on the ferry ride to Watson's Bay.
Fish and chips at Doyle's,
oranges from the local grocer,
a game of tag along the boardwalk.

Synapse: the gap where ships enter
from distant ports.

Li Bai's poem to the solitary
lute player; and Du Fu,
hair grown thin,
welcome mat withdrawn
for all but the closest friends,
remembering Li Bai from world's end.

Two strings, chalk dust
covering the cylindrical base
of the sound box.

The penny drops.

Distance. Departure. Relentless
pounding of the surf.

Basho's road apples

THE PRIZE

What we don't need, the faces seem to say,
is another tourist with aching heart
and counterweights for feet. I inch past
twisted girders, photographic
evidence and charred relics of the A-bomb
exhibit, then leave to place a salmon-coloured rose
on the monument to Sadako. Six hundred
and forty-four folded paper cranes
could not protect her from white cells
warring in her blood.

Light moves through the exposed
struts of the shattered Dome.
A young girl reads a novel by the river
where a string of rental boats fan out
in the confused current. I can't stop thinking
of Akiko Sato, who died nursing her infant
and left nothing but a slip bearing marks
of black rain. Or the boy survived
only by a metal clasp and scrap of leather
on a pedestal. The Japanese character
embossed on Akira Sakanoue's belt buckle
resembles a beetle. I carry my rough approximation
back through the gleaming downtown,
where shops are full of Italian silks
and the pedestrian crosswalks are playing
a computerized version of "Coming through the Rye."

The clerk at the hotel smiles at my calligraphy
and draws the correct version in an upright position
in the margins of my notebook. *Shou*,
she pronounces. But what does it mean,
I ask, knowing the two characters for the city,
hiro and *shima*, mean broad island. She's
as efficient as she is beautiful, flesh and bones
so palpably there beneath the immaculate folds
of the uniform. *If a body kiss a body,*
need a body cry. She checks her dictionary,
smiles again. Just as I thought,
she says, turning the open pages towards me,
the character, in English, means *prize.*

O, Akira, Akiko, I languish in the body
and its fires. If I were a Buddhist,
I'd say, without hesitation, show me the road
that leads beyond desire, or
settle for silence. But I see a desperate
paper-wager, a young mother
yearning to give suck, and a boy
so anxious to serve in the Emperor's
demolition squad — belt buckle
shined, kamikaze of the dust brigade —
he scrubs his small round face until it hurts.

One word after another, reaching out
unstable as molecules, able to take
just so much heat. A spit
of moisture whistles
briefly in the kiln,
is gone.

READING AKIO CHIDA'S TRANSLATIONS
OF THE POEMS OF TOSHIKO TAKADA
ON THE TRAIN FROM HIROSHIMA
TO YOKOHAMA

She understood the sisterhood
of suffering and saw the Band-Aid
on a boy in Paris as a badge
of honour.
              Her finest discriminations
were made on rainy days
under an umbrella.
Comfort of a dead mother's
thin grey hands, faint unreal goodbyes
of those who've yet to learn
what that word signifies.

Melancholy inspired by desert heat
and a donkey, time passing as it does
outside the train window,
mists of Okayama, brown tile roofs
streaking past to disappear
in the dark of tunnels.
                        Poems
so transparent you can feel the ghosts
of children pass through them,
children you might have seen approaching

the bank building where the man
left his shadow forever
on the stone steps, or skipping
along the T-shape of the Aioi Bridge
that morning as the sun withdrew
its savings
from the dazzling water.

INSTALLING THE SQUEAK IN
THE SHOGUN'S FLOOR

Sushitsugu guides me through Osaka Castle
as light retreats from the ancient city.

He began to study literature in French
but *Wuthering Heights* converted him

to English. He says it was the seriousness,
the moral weight, attracted him

to Bronte. Perhaps, post-war, he saw
himself in Heathcliff, pensive, solitary,

peering in the windows of the Grange.
He ushers me through the gates

of the castle, its vast stones
dragged from distant regions

of Japan, describes stages of attack,
possession, restoration. Tezukayama

Gakuin, his university, stands equally
aloof from the commercial bustle

of Osaka, a safe haven for daughters
of the well-to-do who, in their turn,

cultivate a taste for foreign places,
gothic novels, and dream, perhaps,

Montgomery's Anne, orphaned and besieged
by fierce Atlantic gales, secure at last

and warm within her painted gables.
I'm equally drawn to his shadow world

of contradictions: the deadly vanity
of Mishima, stylized grief

that leaves the self at home in Noh plays
and Kabuki; Basho's shameless

exploitation of his hosts but slavish
recording of roadside particulars.

And how not to admire squeaky
pine floorboards in the corridor

of a Kyoto palace that warn the shogun
of an enemy's approach?

All light has fled. Enabling fictions
make us what we are.

IN THE BELLY OF THE BUDDHA

I'm talking with Toshiko Tsutsumi
in the belly of the great bronze Buddha
of Kamakura, carted here, then struck
by a *tsunami,* its protective structures

swept into the sea. She's a tidal wave
in her own right, sweeping over each class
of young women at Oberin, taking them out
over their heads for perhaps the first time.

I'm beginning to like it in here, so much
tidier than Jonah's watery ordeal,
swimming in fish guts and intestinal acid,
trying without success to flee God. Just

as I think I'm being digested, absorbed,
western habits and all, the self intrudes
insistent as rain. Outside, our voices
are heard by four tourists from Toledo

who are convinced the Buddha is
bonkers, suffering a split personality
or unable to distinguish his *yin* from his *yang.*
We discuss children, economics, how

the youngest hang around home so long
they think the house and property
belong to them. I may be in the Buddha,
but I'm no insider. Toshiko tells me

it's not proper to use first names so casually
in Japan, pays my fare into the temple grounds,
and purchases brochures for each exhibit.
The sea, more than a kilometre distant,

sloshes in my cochlea. Light filtered
through the welder's joins and orifices
of the Buddha washes clean my land-locked
spirit. Mind empties. O Professor T., teach me.

BASHO'S ROAD APPLES

1. Zen Garden, Kyoto

Rivers of crushed white
stone, islands for the mind to
navigate. Beware!

2. Japanese New Year

One hundred and eight
sins: so much for the western
poet still to learn.

3. World According to Soza

Water fills bamboo
until the point of balance
has been reached; then, *bong!*

4. Current State of Religion in Japan

Quick glance at temple
blossoms, then we skedaddle
for tea and sake.

5. Foreign Manners

Hotel. Wedding guests
arrive, dressed to the nines. My
tasteless flash explodes.

6. Comparative Studies, Hazelton

Akira, so keen
to see totem poles in snow,
his car left the road.

7. August 5, 1945

A thousand gods
assigned to protect children:
8:15, slept in.

Other Books by Gary Geddes

POETRY
Poems (1971)
Rivers Inlet (1972)
Snakeroot (1973)
Letter of the Master of Horse (1973)
War & other measures (1976)
The Acid Test (1980)
The Terracotta Army (1984)
Changes of State (1986)
Hong Kong (1987)
No Easy Exit (1989)
Light of Burning Towers (1990)
Girl by the Water (1994)
The Perfect Cold Warrior (1995)
Active Trading: Selected Poems 1970-1995 (1996)

FICTION
The Unsettling of the West (1986)

DRAMA
Les Maudits Anglais (1984)

TRANSLATION
I Didn't Notice the Mountain Growing Dark (1986),
poems of Li Pai and Tu Fu, translated with the assistance of George Liang

CRITICISM
Conrad's Later Novels (1980)

ANTHOLOGIES
20th-Century Poetry and Poetics (1969, 1973, 1985, 1996)
15 Canadian Poets Times 2 (1971, 1977, 1988)
Skookum Wawa: Writings of the Canadian Northwest (1975)
Divided We Stand (1977)
The Inner Ear (1983)
Chinada: Memoirs of the Gang of Seven (1983)
Vancouver: Soul of a City (1986)
Compañeros: Writings about Latin America (1990)
The Art of Short Fiction: An International Anthology (1992)